SCOOBY-DOO! and YOU:

A Collect the Clues Mystery

THE CASE OF THE DOUGHY CREATURE

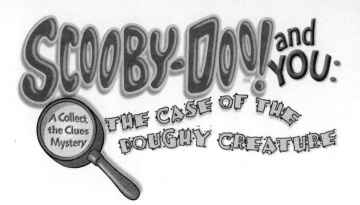

SCOOBY-DOO! and YOU: THE CASE OF THE DOUGHY CREATURE

A Collect the Clues Mystery

By Jenny Markas

SCHOLASTIC INC.

New York   Toronto   London   Auckland   Sydney
Mexico City   New Delhi   Hong Kong

For Laureen and Caribou

ISBN 0-439-21752-0

12 11 10 9 8 7 6 5 4 3 2 1   0 1 2 3 4 5/0

Cover and interior illustrations by Duendes del Sur
Cover and interior design by Madalina Stefan

Printed in the U.S.A.

First Scholastic printing, October 2000

"**M**an, am I glad to see you!" Shaggy waves and grins as you walk into the Chinese restaurant. He's sitting at a booth with Fred, Velma, Daphne, and Scooby. The place is decorated with a dragon motif, and the walls and chairs are a deep red with gold trim. It feels cozy — and it smells delicious.

Shaggy hands you a menu as you pull out a chair and sit down. "With you here, we can order even more dishes to share. Hey, do you like egg foo young? Or maybe some fried rice? And they make a great chow mein here . . ."

1

"Shaggy, take it easy," Fred says. "There'll be enough food for everyone."

"Reg rolls!" insists Scooby.

Velma laughs. "Yes, of course we'll order egg rolls, Scooby." She turns to you. "You'd think these two never ate in their lives." She shakes her head. "I don't know how they could be hungry at all. They just finished gobbling up tons of pastries at the bakery where we solved our last mystery."

"Rum, rum," Scooby says, smiling and rubbing his tummy.

"Those eclairs were, like, the best." Shaggy closes his eyes and smiles happily, remembering. "The cream-puffs were excellent, too."

"Rookies!" Scooby says.

"Too true, Scoob." Shaggy nods. "The coo-kies were, like, the best ever."

"Personally, it'll be a while before I can face any more sweet treats,"

Daphne says, rolling her eyes. "That was the best bakery I ever went to."

"Except for the Doughy Creature," Velma says with a shiver. "Jinkies! I lost my appetite when he was around. Good thing we solved that mystery and made sure he'll never show up again."

Fred notices that you look interested. "Want to hear more about the mystery at the bakery?" he asks. "It's all in our Clue Keeper. You can read through it and try to solve the mystery yourself."

"That's right," Velma says, showing you the Clue Keeper. "I kept the notes this time. Lucky for you, since I have the best handwriting! Anyway, everything's in there. All the clues, all the suspects, everything."

Daphne nods. "You'll be able to tell when you're meeting a suspect because there will be spooky eyes there." She opens the Clue Keeper and shows you 👁 👁 . "And when you see a flashlight 🔦 , you'll know you've found a clue."

"We even help you organize your thinking," Fred says, "with a list of questions at the end of each Clue Keeper entry. Got a pencil? You can write down the answers in your own Clue Keeper."

You're ready to get to work on solving the mystery, but just then the food arrives. Five waiters, each carrying a huge tray, start putting down platters and bowls until the pile of food nearly covers the table.

Shaggy smiles contentedly. "Mysteries are great, but food comes first. Like, let's dig in!" he says. He grabs an egg roll and starts munching away. Scooby starts slurping noodles. You smile and shrug, reaching for the platter of chow mein. It sounds like this mystery will take some thinking, and you might as well keep your strength up!

Clue Keeper Entry 1

"Wow, man," Shaggy said, surveying the cases full of treats. "Like, this is great!" He sniffed the air, appreciating the sweet smell of baking.

"*Merci!*" said a short, round man with a big, droopy black mustache. He was wearing a starched white jacket and a high, puffy white hat. "I mean, thank you. I am so glad you appreciate fine baking." He came around from behind the counter to greet us. "So lovely to see you again, Mademoiselle Velma," he said, bending to kiss my hand.

Monsieur Pamplemousse is a real

charmer. And an incredible pastry chef, too! He is French, and his bakery, Le Grand Chien, is the best. When I want a sweet treat, I always go there. My friends and I had just driven over in the Mystery Machine. We were looking for an afternoon snack — but we got more than we bargained for.

"I am so glad you brought your friends," Monsieur Pamplemousse told me. "I can always use more business."

The place did seem kind of empty. The last time I had been there, it was packed with customers. But this time, we were just about the only ones there. "You used to be so busy," I said.

He nodded sadly. "Not anymore," he answered. "Now I'm afraid I may not be able to pay my rent much longer."

"But why — " Fred began.

Monsieur Pamplemousse raised his hands to stop the question. "Never mind, never mind," he said. "I don't want to talk about it. How about a nice treat? Let's forget our troubles with a pastry, shall we?"

Shaggy's eyes lit up. So did Scooby's. "Roh, roy!" he said excitedly.

"I'd like one of those, and one of those, and, like, four of those," Shaggy said, pointing at the beautiful creations in the case. There were chocolate cookies and muffins and fruit tarts and pastries made of millions of layers of dough. A separate case held beautifully decorated cakes, covered with icing flowers in every color of the rainbow. Loaves of bread in all shapes and sizes filled baskets on the high shelves behind the counter. Everything looked delicious.

Monsieur Pamplemousse laughed. "Slow down," he said as he headed behind the counter to take our order. "These pastries are made to be enjoyed slowly, one at a time."

Shaggy looked disappointed. "But they all look so good!" he said.

"They *are* good," said a man who had just come in. He was looking into one of the cases. "Much better than I can make." He shook his head. "My name is Stanley Mason, and I'm a baker, too.  I have my own place down the street. But I've never been able to create pastries like these. If I could, I know I would be a rich man." He gazed longingly at a row of eclairs. "I'd sure like one of those," he said, "but I'm on a diet." He patted his stomach, which looked pretty flat to me. Then he caught Monsieur Pamplemousse's eye. "Just a roll, please," he said. "No butter."

Monsieur Pamplemousse shook his head disapprovingly. "What about one of these delicious walnut cookies?" he asked, pointing to a tray of tempting treats.

Stanley Mason frowned and shook his head. "They look wonderful, but I'm allergic to nuts. I could get very sick if I ate anything with nuts in it. I'll just have the roll."

Monsieur Pamplemousse shrugged. He pulled a roll out of a basket brimming with bread, put it in a small bag, and handed it to Stanley Mason. He took the money Stanley Mason gave him and put it into the cash register. Then he turned back to Scooby and Shaggy, rubbing his hands with delight. "So," he said. "What will it be? A napoleon, perhaps? Or a mousse tart?"

"Roose?" Scooby asked, looking alarmed.

"Mousse," Monsieur Pamplemousse replied, "not *moose*. It is like pudding, only much, much better."

"Rousse!" Scooby agreed, nodding eagerly. Monsieur Pamplemousse smiled and reached into the case.

"Like, mousse sounds good to me, too," Shaggy told the baker. "And . . . um . . ."

Monsieur Pamplemousse smiled. "I see you are looking at the lemon tarts," he said. "A very wise choice." He added another mousse tart and two lemon tarts to the tray he was holding. "And what can I get for the rest of you?"

Fred, Daphne, and I gazed into the case. It was hard to choose, since everything looked so good. Monsieur Pamplemousse knows how to show off his pastries. They were arranged in neat rows in the clean, bright cases. The fruit tarts looked like little jewels, and the cookies made my mouth water. I chose a chocolate chip cookie. Fred picked a croissant (that's a buttery, flaky roll), and Daphne went for an eclair like the one Stanley Mason had wanted.

Monsieur Pamplemousse piled everything onto a tray. "Wonderful, wonderful," he said. "Why don't you take this over to one of the tables and enjoy your snack?" He gestured toward the dining area of the bakery, where several small tables were positioned near a large, sunny window. Stanley Mason was sitting at one of them, taking bites out of his roll. "I will join you in a few minutes. After you've eaten, perhaps you would enjoy a tour of the bakery."

"We'd love that!" I exclaimed.

He handed the tray to me. "Well, then, *bon appetit!*" He smiled. "That means 'Happy eating.'"

"Like, I'm always happy when I'm eating," Shaggy said, following me closely as I carried the tray to a table.

"**C**an you believe this pastry shop? Like, I've never seen so many yummy-looking things in one place before. Anyway, did you catch the 👁 👁 back on page 8? Great! That means you can probably answer these questions:"

1. What is the suspect's name?

2. What does he do for a living?

3. Why would he be interested in shutting down Le Grand Chien?

"Once you've answered, help yourself to a cookie (or two!)."

Clue Keeper Entry 2

We pulled up chairs to one of the tables, and I unloaded our goodies from the tray. Then we all sat down to eat.

"You're lucky to have a baker like Monsieur Pamplemousse for a friend," Shaggy said to me, after he'd taken his first huge bite of lemon tart.

"I know," I said. "Remember the birthday cake he made me last year? It had five different layers. Chocolate, vanilla, lemon, raspberry, and strawberry. And it was decorated with huge pink roses."

"I don't understand why this place isn't

packed," Daphne said. "I mean, this food is delicious!" She licked her fingers (eclair-eating can be a messy business) and smiled contentedly.

"There's something weird about that," Fred agreed. "I mean, who wouldn't want pastries like these? What could be keeping people away?"

Just then, the little bell over the door rang as someone pushed it open. A tall man with wire-rimmed glasses walked in. He was carrying a briefcase, and he had a hopeful look on his face.

Behind the counter, Monsieur Pample-mousse smiled. "*Bon jour, Monsieur Jamieson.* What can I get for you?" he asked.

"I'll have a cup of coffee, and do you have the apricot pastries today?" asked the man.

Monsieur Pamplemousse shook his head a little sadly. "No, no apricot pastries today," he said. "Not for a while. The ingredients are just too expensive."

"But they're my favorite!" said the man. Monsieur Pamplemousse shrugged. "I'm sorry," he said. "Can I offer you something else?"

"Let me think about it," answered the man, looking over the pastries in the case.

"I'll be right back," said Monsieur Pamplemousse. "I have some bread that must come out of the oven right now." He darted back into the kitchen.

Shaggy gestured toward the customer. "Hey, man," he said, "I recommend the elk tarts."

"Elk?" asked the man.

"I mean mousse," Shaggy said, blushing.

The man shook his head. "I'm afraid that if I can't have my apricot tarts I don't want anything," he said. "I keep telling Monsieur Pamplemousse that. If he won't make my tarts again, he'll be sorry."

"What do you mean?" Fred asked.

"I happen to be the landlord of this bakery," the man replied. "My name's Ingo

15

Jamieson, and I own lots of real estate in this area. Lately, Monsieur Pamplemousse can't always pay his rent. I have been forgiving, but if he has so few customers that he can't afford to make my tarts I don't know how much longer I can put up with losing money on this space. I can rent it out just like that," he snapped his fingers, "to someone else who will pay me every month. I've warned him, but he won't listen."

"Maybe you can find something else you like to eat!" I said, thinking that I would hate to see my friend lose his bakery.

"Rookie?" Scooby offered hopefully.

"He thinks you might like a cookie," Shaggy translated.

"No, thanks." Mr. Jamieson picked up his briefcase and the cup of coffee Monsieur Pamplemousse had poured for him. "If I can't have my apricot pastries, I don't want anything." Annoyed, he walked over to sit at a table in the corner and drink his coffee.

We just looked at each other and shrugged. He didn't know what he was missing.

Fred's Mystery-Solving Tips

"**D**id you happen to notice the 👁 👁 on page 15? Good going. Pick up your pencil and answer some questions about this suspect."

1. What is the suspect's name?

2. What does he do for a living?

3. Why would he be interested in shutting down Le Grand Chien?

Clue Keeper Entry 3

"Jinkies!" I said. "I don't understand how he could walk away without getting *something* here." I took another bite of my cookie. The chocolate chips melted in my mouth. It was just about the best cookie I'd ever had.

"I don't mind,"Shaggy said. "It just means there's more left for us." He gazed at the display case. He still looked hungry.

"Look at all those people walking by," said Fred, gesturing out the window. "Why don't they come inside for a treat?"

"I saw a few people glance in," Daphne

said. "But they looked kind of scared or something. Then they just kept walking."

Shaggy scratched his chin. "What could possibly be scary about a bakery?"

"I can't imagine," Fred said. "But it does seem like there's something going on. If only Monsieur Pamplemousse would talk about it, maybe we could help."

Just then, the bell over the door jingled again. We looked up to see another customer walk in, a blond man in a business suit, carrying a briefcase and wearing sunglasses. He looked around, as if checking to see who had seen him come in. He did not take off the sunglasses.

The man walked over to the case and began to lick his lips as he looked over the pastries. "Oh, my, oh, my," I heard him mutter. He checked behind him again.

"*Bon jour*, Monsieur Dewhurst!" Monsieur Pamplemousse called as he bustled out of the kitchen to see who had come in.

"Shh! Shhh!" the man whispered. "You know I don't want anyone to know I come in here."

Monsieur Pamplemousse just laughed. "You love fine pastry. That is nothing to be ashamed of!" he said.

Mr. Dewhurst looked upset. He shook his head. "But I should be eating my own pastries."

"Yummy Crullers?" Monsieur Pamplemousse asked. "Those are not pastries. Those are doughnuts for people who don't know anything about fine baking."

Mr. Dewhurst started to say something.

Monsieur Pamplemousse held up his hands. "I know, I know, your franchise makes plenty of money. You sell a thousand doughnuts a day. You could open another store in this area and sell a thousand more. But try this." He reached into the case and pulled out a creampuff. "Tell me that isn't ten times more delicious than your best doughnut."

Mr. Dewhurst put down his briefcase. He

took a bite of the creampuff and closed his eyes, smiling. "It's delicious," he said. "Just delicious."

Monsieur Pamplemousse nodded. He gestured to us. "You see these young people?" he asked. "They appreciate delicious pastry as well." He introduced us.

Mr. Dewhurst smiled nervously.

"I like Yummy Crullers, too!" Shaggy told him. "I wish there were a Yummy Crullers store right nearby."

"Do you think we could sell lots of doughnuts in this town?" Mr. Dewhurst asked, interested.

"Oh, yeah, man," Shaggy answered. "Like, definitely."

Mr. Dewhurst nodded thoughtfully. "That's what I think, too." He picked up the rest of the creampuff and sat down at a table to finish it off. I saw him take out a little notebook and make some notes as he ate. He still hadn't taken off his sunglasses! 👁 👁

22

"I wonder if you noticed the 👀 on page 22. Did you? Great. That means you've identified another suspect. Try to figure out more about him by answering these questions in your Clue Keeper."

1. What is the suspect's name?

2. What does he do for a living?

3. Why would he be interested in shutting down Le Grand Chien?

"Good job! You're on your way to solving this mystery."

23

Clue Keeper Entry 4

By then, a few more customers had come into the store. I saw two women come in. One of them was carrying a baby. "Are you sure it's safe?" I heard her ask her friend.

"It's only a story," her friend answered. "A silly story about a monster in a bakery. How could it be true?" They walked over to look into the display case.

I glanced over at my friends to see if they'd heard. Sure enough, Daphne's eyes were round.

"A monster?" Fred asked.

"In a bakery?" Shaggy asked.

I gulped. "Jinkies! No wonder this place isn't so busy anymore."

We didn't have a chance to talk about it more because Monsieur Pamplemousse chose that moment to speak up. "There is no monster in my bakery," he announced. "I invite all my customers for a tour of the baking area, so I can prove this to you. Please join me."

The two women looked nervous, but interested. I saw Stanley Mason jump to his feet. It figured. As a baker himself, he'd have to be interested in seeing Monsieur Pamplemousse's kitchen. Ingo Jamieson shrugged. "I've seen the place before," he said, "since I own it. But it's always fun to take a tour with Monsieur Pamplemousse." A couple of other customers looked ready to join the tour as well.

I gulped again. If there was a monster back in the bakery, did we really want to meet it?

But Shaggy didn't wait for me to answer. "Like, wow!" he said eagerly. "I always wanted to go behind the scenes at a bakery."

25

Monsieur Pamplemousse smiled. "Wonderful," he said. "Follow me." He led us behind the counter, through a door, and around a corner, and suddenly we were in a brightly lit room that smelled even more delicious than the store part of the bakery. There were high, steel tables for rolling out dough, and shelves stacked with cake pans and cookie tins. A big red notebook with the word RECIPES sat in the corner of one shelf. I saw rolling racks that held trays of just-baked pastries, cookies, and cakes that must have been cooling before they could be put out in the case. And a giant mixing machine stood in one corner, mixing a huge batch of dough.

"That is bread dough," Monsieur Pamplemousse explained. "Here is what it looks like when it's just mixed," he went on, showing us a bowl with a small mound of dough in it. "And here," he opened the door of a warming oven, "is how it looks after the yeast has worked to make it rise." He pulled out a bowl of the same size, which was now overflowing with dough.

"Wow!" Daphne said.

Monsieur Pamplemousse went on to show us the ovens where everything was baked, as well as the huge walk-in refrigerators where pastry ingredients were kept. Not everyone was paying attention. I noticed some of the people in the tour wandering off on their own to look over the racks of pastry again or peek into the warming ovens. Monsieur Pamplemousse didn't seem to mind.

As we walked by one of the tables, I noticed a bunch of cookie-cutters, and right next to them was a little model of a person, all made out of dough. It was so cute, with its

round head and little round body. I wanted
to go over to look at it, but then I was dis-
tracted by a waft of the most delicious smell.

"Mmm, what's cooking?" Daphne asked.

"That is a *gateau chocolat*," answered
Monsieur Pamplemousse.

"That sounds fancy," Mr. Jamieson said.

"No, no," Monsieur Pamplemousse shook
his head. "It is just chocolate cake."

"*Just* chocolate cake?" Shaggy and Scooby
exchanged a look. Scooby licked his lips.

"We can have some after our tour," Monsieur Pamplemousse said. "It should be done
by then." He opened the door of a huge oven
and peeked inside. "Yes, I think it will be done."

I stood on tiptoes to look inside. Just

then, I heard Daphne gasp behind me. I whirled around to see a giant version of the little dough man I'd just seen on the table. He had grown, just like the bread dough. He was taller than me, taller than Fred. How had he grown that fast? He was huge and puffy and looked doughlike. His cute little round body wasn't so cute anymore. If he grabbed one of us, we'd be stuck in his arms. It was like a nightmare. He raised his arms and started toward me. His doughy feet stuck to the floor with each giant step he took, but it didn't seem to slow him down much. "Help!" I cried, running toward the door that led to the sales counter.

Clue Keeper Entry 5

"Zoinks!" Shaggy yelled. "That must be the monster they were talking about! He's, like, a Doughy Creature!"

The woman with a baby gave a little shriek.

"Don't scream, please," Monsieur Pamplemousse begged. "The other customers will be frightened."

The Doughy Creature was moving toward us, slowly but surely. Scooby, staring at the creature, took one too many steps backward and fell right into the bowl of the giant mixer. "Rikes!" he cried as he went round and round. "Relp!"

Daphne grabbed Scooby and helped him out of the mixer. He was covered with dough.

Then Fred sneaked up behind the Doughy Creature, pushed him into the bowl, and turned up the speed. The creature howled as he was spun round and round.

"Let's get out of here!" Fred said. "Follow me!"

We all ran out into the salesroom. The customers in the store took one look at our frightened faces and pushed their way out the door.

Monsieur Pamplemousse was wringing his hands. "You see?" he asked. "Nobody wants to come to my bakery because of that monster. What can I do?"

"Don't worry," I told him. "Now I understand why you've lost so much business. We can help you. If we can figure out where that monster came from, maybe we can make sure he never shows up again."

"Could you do that?" Monsieur Pample-mousse asked. "If you could, I would be grateful forever. I would offer you a lifetime supply of pastry."

"Monsieur Pamplemousse," Shaggy said, stepping up and putting his hand over his heart, "Like, say no more. We are at your service."

Scooby, who still had bits of dough clinging to his fur, stepped up next to Shaggy and put his paw over his heart, too.

"Okay," I said to the others. "I think there's something fishy about this monster. How about if we split up and look for clues? Shaggy and Scooby and I can look around in the kitchen."

"That sounds great," Fred said. "Daphne and I can look around in the store and the dining area."

"We can meet at the table where we were

sitting before," Daphne suggested. "Just be sure to be careful. That Doughy Creature could create a pretty sticky situation!"

"Nothing can come between me and, like, a lifetime supply of free pastry!" Shaggy said. "Let's go!"

Shaggy and Scooby and I walked into the kitchen and looked around. The kitchen was quiet and clean. There was no sign of the Doughy Creature. I sighed with relief. "Where do we start?" I wondered, looking around.

"I guess we check to see if anything's missing or, like, out of place," Shaggy said. "Hmm, was this cookie here before?" He held up a big peanut-butter cookie that had been sitting on a plate on one of the work-tables. "I think I'd better check if it's okay," he added, taking a bite. "Mmpph," he said, a second later, with his mouth full. "Nothing wrong with this cookie. Like, nothing at all."

Scooby gave Shaggy a hopeful look. Shaggy grinned at him and gave him the last bite of cookie. "Rmmm," Scooby said happily.

"Jinkies!" I cried, just then. "Look what's missing!" I pointed to the shelf over in the corner. Before, there had been a big red RECIPE book up there. Now it was gone. "How will Monsieur Pamplemousse be able to make all these delicious things without his recipes?"

"And, like, who would steal something like that?" Shaggy asked, scratching his head. "That doesn't make much sense."

Velma's Mystery-Solving Tips

"Did you notice the on page 34? Now you've got your first clue. You might want to write down the answers to these questions in your Clue Keeper."

1. What clue did you find in this entry?

2. Why is this clue important?

3. Which of the suspects might have been responsible for this clue?

35

Clue Keeper Entry 6

"I can't believe somebody took Monsieur Pamplemousse's recipe book," I said.

"Like, it's, tragic," Shaggy agreed. "But maybe he has most of his recipes memorized anyway," he added hopefully.

"Let's see if we can find anything else missing," I said. I started to walk around the kitchen, checking all the tables and shelves. I even peeked into the giant bins of flour, and looked into the warming ovens. We had to do a complete search if we wanted to find clues.

Meanwhile, Shaggy and Scooby were

looking over the rolling racks that held trays of pastries.

"Look, Scoob," Shaggy said. "There's a little piece missing out of this creampuff. Do you think it's a clue?"

Scooby took a close look. Very close. So close that some cream ended up on the tip of his nose. In the next second, the creampuff had disappeared into Scooby's mouth.

"Oops," Shaggy grinned. "Like, so much for that piece of evidence." He helped himself to the next creampuff on the tray. "I know Monsieur Pamplemousse wouldn't want us to be working on, like, an empty stomach." He wolfed down the creampuff and licked his lips. "In fact, I'm pretty sure he'd want us to know all about every pastry in this place. Otherwise, how can we figure out the mystery?" He began to pull out each rack, helping himself — and Scooby — to one of each of all the different pastries that were cooling.

"Mmm, wow, try this one!" Shaggy cried, pointing to some apple strudel.

"Rexcellent!" Scooby agreed, after taking a huge bite.

"And this one!" Shaggy reached onto another rack. "Hey, look! This pastry has apricots on it. Almonds, too. Yum! I wonder if it's the kind Ingo Jamieson likes. Maybe Monsieur Pamplemousse, like, was going to surprise him with it."

Shaggy checked the rack. "That's funny," he said. "Hey, Velma," he called to me, "there's one missing. And I didn't take it!" Did you?"

"No," I replied from across the kitchen. Scooby and Shaggy were both so focused on the pastries that they didn't notice a noise

behind them. Suddenly, two huge blobby hands reached out and grabbed Scooby and Shaggy by the shoulders. Shaggy told me later that he could smell the Doughy Creature's sweet breath because the monster was so close.

"Zoinks!" Shaggy cried. "It's the Doughy Creature! Run for your life!" He ducked and pulled away from the creature's grasp. The creature seemed bigger than ever. "Come on, Scoob!" Shaggy ran toward a big metal door, hoping to find his way out of the kitchen. Scooby dashed after him. The Doughy Creature was right on their heels.

Shaggy yanked the door open.

"No!" I cried. "That's the walk-in refrigerator!"

But it was too late. In his rush to get away from the creature, Shaggy jumped inside, pulled Scooby in with him, and slammed the door behind them.

The Doughy Creature pounded on the door with his huge fists, howling loudly.

I ran in the opposite direction, toward the sales counter, the dining room — and safety. Shaggy and Scooby were going to be cold, but at least they were safe from the creature.

Shaggy and Scooby's Mystery-Solving Tips

"Like, we were freezing in that fridge! But you must be happy, since you found a clue , right? Try answering these questions in your Clue Keeper:"

1. What clue did you find in this entry?

2. Which suspect do you think might be responsible for the clue?

3. Why would the Doughy Creature be upset about us finding the clue?

Clue Keeper Entry 7

"Fred! Daphne!" I ran out of the kitchen and right into my friends. "You won't believe what happened! The Doughy Creature chased Shaggy and Scooby right into the walk-in refrigerator!"

"Oh, no!" Daphne cried. "That's terrible."

"We'd better go let them out," Fred said.

We started back into the kitchen, but Monsieur Pamplemousse stopped us. "Wait," he said. "What if the creature is still in there? I don't want anyone to get hurt in my bakery."

"Monsieur Pamplemousse is right," Fred said. "We should think about this. How can we rescue Shaggy and Scooby without getting caught ourselves?"

We all thought for a moment. "Jinkies! I know!" I said, remembering the missing pastry. "I have a feeling that the creature likes apricot pastries. What if we leave a tray out in plain sight for him to see? If he's around, he'll pay more attention to them than to us."

"Excellent plan," Monsieur Pamplemousse nodded. "I have a tray of them right here. I felt sorry for Mr. Jamieson, so I made several batches." He pulled out a tray from beneath the counter. Sure enough, they were the same ones Shaggy and Scooby and I had seen in the kitchen, complete with almonds and apricots.

Fred took it. "Great. We'll put this in plain sight, somewhere far from the fridge. Then we can let Scooby and Shaggy out of there."

We walked into the kitchen together, looking all around for the creature. He was nowhere in sight, though I did see some doughy marks on the floor where he'd walked.

Fred put the tray of pastries on one of the worktables. "Mmm, those apricot pastries sure do look good!" he said loudly.

"Apricot? My favorite!" Daphne echoed.

If the creature was around, and if I was right about his taste in pastries, he wasn't going to be paying any attention to us. I headed straight for the walk-in fridge and threw the door open.

"Hey, what's up?" Shaggy asked. He was shivering, and his arms were covered in goosebumps from the cold, but he was smiling.

And eating a big bowl of cookie dough.

"Ruh-roh," Scooby said, pulling his paw out of the bowl when he realized they'd been caught.

"We, like, found this stuff on one of the shelves," Shaggy explained. "We thought we'd better keep eating, just to keep warm."

"Sure, sure," Fred said with a smile. "Well, as long as you're safe. Come on out of there and we'll tell you about the clue we found."

"We found some, too!" I said.

We all trooped back out into the dining area and sat down around our old table to compare notes. I told Daphne and Fred about the clues we had found. Then Daphne showed me a small notebook and a tape mea-  sure. "I found these on the floor near one of the display cases," she said. "Look at the notes inside."

I looked at the first page. "Forty-eight inches, at four inches per doughnut, equals twelve doughnuts per row," I read. "That's strange. Monsieur Pamplemousse doesn't even bake doughnuts."

"I think it's time to get to the bottom of things in this bakery," Fred said. "I have a feeling somebody might have 'cooked up' this creature. It's time to trap the Doughy Creature and find out who he really is."

"We're betting you spotted the 🔦 on page 45. Do you have a feeling we're getting closer to solving the mystery? You can help by answering the following questions:"

1. What clue did you find in this entry?

2. What does it have to do with the mystery at the bakery?

3. Which suspect might have left this clue?

47

Clue Keeper Entry 8

What was the best way to trap the Doughy Creature? Fred had an idea. "The Doughy Creature wants to shut down Monsieur Pamplemousse's bakery. If he thinks the bakery is getting more business than ever, he'll show up to try to stop it."

"That makes sense," Shaggy said, nodding. "So how do we make it look like there's more business?"

"By pretending that Monsieur Pamplemousse had to hire two new pastry chefs," Fred said, producing two big puffy chef's hats. "You and Scooby will disguise yourselves as chefs and pretend to be working in the kitchen. That will bring the Doughy Creature around, and the rest of us can trap him and find out who he really is."

Shaggy was shaking his head. "Like, this sounds too dangerous to me."

"Ruh-ruh," Scooby said, holding out both paws and shaking his head, too.

"Come on, Shaggy," I said. "Think of all the pastries you can eat while you're working."

Shaggy's eyes lit up. "On second thought . . ." he said.

Scooby still looked unsure.

"How about it, Scooby?" Daphne asked. "Will you do it for a Scooby Snack?"

Scooby folded his arms and stuck his chin in the air.

"How about two Scooby Snacks?" I asked.

Scooby opened one eye, as if he were considering my offer.

"Two Scooby Snacks and a seven-layer chocolate cake baked just for you!" Monsieur Pamplemousse put in.

That did the trick. "Rokay!" Scooby's eyes lit up and he nodded eagerly. Daphne tossed him two Scooby Snacks and he gobbled them down.

Then he and Shaggy put on the chef's hats and matching white chef's coats. The final touch? Matching big black mustaches, just like Monsieur Pamplemousse's. Then we all headed into the kitchen. Scooby and Shaggy took up their places at a worktable while the rest of us hid behind the cooling racks.

"When the Doughy Creature appears, we'll roll these racks toward him and trap him in a pastry jail cell!" Fred said. "Then we can find out if he's a creature — or a criminal."

"I sure hope your plan works," Shaggy said nervously.

"Trust us," Daphne said.

Shaggy shrugged. "Like, okay," he said. He started to knead some bread dough that was on the worktable. "Like, here I go, being a pastry chef," he continued in a louder voice. "We need lots of extra bread and pastry for all those new customers!"

Scooby joined in the act, rolling dough while Shaggy sprinkled flour over the work-table.

Suddenly, there was a noise from behind one of the ovens, and the Doughy Creature appeared just behind Shaggy and Scooby. Large and puffy with arms outstretched, he lumbered toward Shaggy.

Shaggy didn't notice. He was getting very involved in his bread dough. "You know, Scoob," he said, "this is, like, a lot of fun. I wouldn't mind being a real pastry chef!"

Just then, the Doughy Creature took one step closer.

"Wait a second, I smell dough," Shaggy said. He turned to see the creature breathing down his neck. "Aaahhhh!" he cried.

"Now!" yelled Fred.

We all pushed our racks forward, sur-

rounding the creature in a cage. We'd caught him!

Shaggy and Scooby sighed with relief.

"I think it's time to find out who this creature really is," Fred said. He reached through the racks and grabbed the Doughy Creature's head. He pulled at the dough, and with a sucking sound it came right off. The head was fake!

"More tea?" Daphne asks you as she holds up the teapot. You and the gang have nearly finished all the food Shaggy ordered. Everything was great, especially the egg rolls.

"Sure," you say, putting down the Clue Keeper and holding out your cup.

"Looks like you're done reading my notes," Velma says. "Do you think you're ready to solve the mystery?"

You're not positive, but you say you'll give it a try.

"We'll help," Fred says. "First of all, think

about your suspects. Which of them do you think had a good reason to scare people away from Le Grand Chien?"

"Second," Daphne adds, "which of the suspects might have left the clues that we found?"

"It might help to eliminate some of the suspects, if you can," Velma points out.

"How about a fortune cookie?" Shaggy asks. "Like, it might bring you good luck." He hands you a plate of fortune cookies, and you choose one and break it open.

Your fortune says, *You are close to finding out the truth.* That sounds promising!

"Look over your Clue Keeper one more time," Daphne suggests. "Then, when you're ready, we'll tell you who the Doughy Creature really was."

Zoinks! Can you guess who's behind the Doughy Creature's antics? When you're ready, turn the page to read how the gang solved the mystery.

"It was Mr. Dewhurst, the Yummy Crullers man," Fred says. "He created a costume out of hardened doughnut dough and dressed up like the Doughy Creature to scare people away from Le Grand Chien, because he wanted to open a doughnut store in that space. He stole the recipe book, too, since he wanted to learn how to make good pastries, not just doughnuts. And he couldn't resist grabbing that apricot pastry when nobody was around to see him eating it."

"He wasn't the only suspect who would have liked to close down the bakery," Velma tells you. "Ingo Jamieson had his reasons, too. He could have rented the place in a minute to someone who could pay the rent. We wondered if he might have stolen the recipe book to find out how to make those apricot pastries. And of course he would have snitched the pastry itself because he loved them so much. But why would he be measuring the pastry cases? He's the land-lord and, as he said, he knows everything about his own building."

"And there's a happy ending to that story," Daphne adds. "Business will be up

again now that the creature is gone, and Monsieur Pamplemousse has promised to make the apricot pastries every day for his landlord."

"You probably know that the other suspect was Stanley Mason," says Fred. "He's a baker, too, and he was jealous of Monsieur Pamplemousse's great baking. He's decided to give up pastry-making and concentrate on Italian food instead."

"Even though we thought it might be him at first, because he might have stolen the recipe book and also the apricot pastry, we realized it couldn't be him because he is allergic to nuts, and there were almonds in that pastry," Daphne explains.

"Finally," Fred says, "the clue that tipped

us off was the notebook Mr. Dewhurst left by the display case. He took advantage of everyone being on the kitchen tour to measure the cases and figure out how many doughnuts they would hold. Then he ran into the kitchen to make an appearance as the Doughy Creature — but his big mistake was leaving that notebook behind."

"So, did you figure out the mystery?" Velma asks. "I bet you did, since my notes in our Clue Keeper were so good." She grins at you.

"I'm sure you solved it fast," Daphne says. "But if you didn't, there's always another chance. We're always coming across mysteries to solve."

"Like, she's right," Shaggy says. "But most of them aren't quite as delicious as this one was!" He reaches into a big box on the table and pulls out a huge chocolate cake. "Scooby said he'd like to share this with everybody. It's the cake Monsieur Pamplemousse baked to thank us for saving his bakery." Shaggy cuts four small pieces of the cake and passes them around to you, Fred, Daphne, and Velma. Then he cuts the rest of the cake into two *gigantic* pieces, one for him and one for Scooby.

Scooby takes a huge bite and then looks up with chocolate icing all over his nose. "Rooby-Rooby-Roo!" he says happily.